This edition published by Parragon in 2012
Parragon
Queen Street House
4 Queen Street
Bath BA1 1HE, UK
www.parragon.com

ISBN 978-1-4454-8939-1

Printed in China

Alice in Wonderland

Based on the story by Lewis Carroll
Illustrated by Amanda Gulliver

Bath · New York · Singapore · Hong Kong · Cologne · Delhi
Melbourne · Amsterdam · Johannesburg · Auckland · Shenzhen

Alice was sitting with her sister on the grass by a river bank, when a White Rabbit ran past.

"Oh dear!
I shall be too late!"
said the Rabbit.

Alice followed the Rabbit and found herself falling down a rabbit hole.

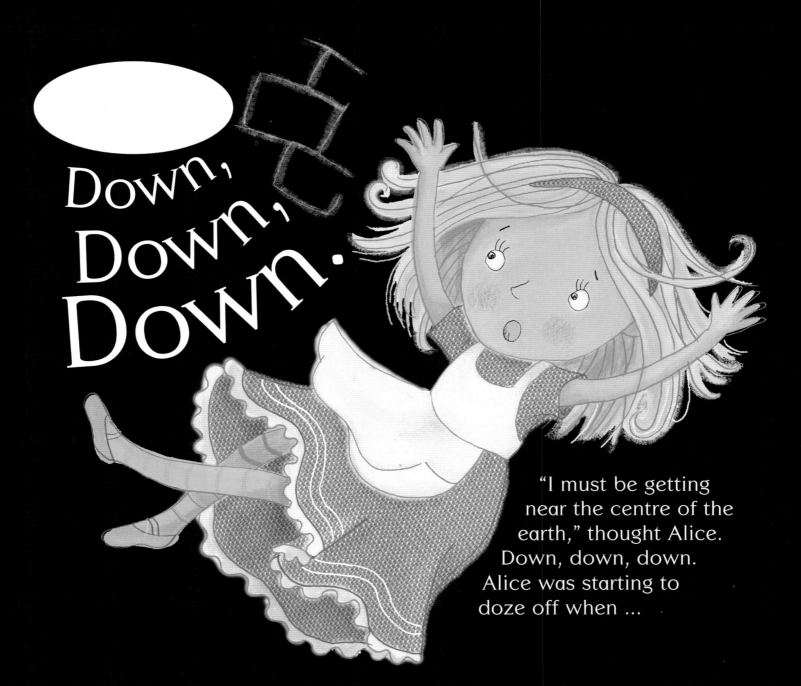

Down, Down, Down.

"I must be getting near the centre of the earth," thought Alice. Down, down, down. Alice was starting to doze off when ...

THUMP!

She landed in a heap and the fall was over.

Alice found herself in a hall lined with doors. Next to one of the doors was a glass table with a key on it. Alice tried the key in all of the doors, but it wouldn't open any of them.

Then Alice found a tiny door hidden behind a curtain. The key opened the door, but she couldn't fit through it.

Alice went back to the table and found a little bottle labelled

'DRINK ME'.

When she drank it, she started to shrink!

She was now small enough to fit through the door, but the key was on the table, and she couldn't reach it!

EAT ME

Then she spotted a small cake, with 'EAT ME' written on it in currants.
"Curiouser and curiouser!" she said.

7

When she ate the cake she grew so big, her head hit the roof! Alice cried until there was a pool of tears all around her. Then the White Rabbit ran past with a pair of gloves and a fan. The Rabbit dropped them when it saw Alice. She picked them up and fanned herself.

The fan made her shrink!

Alice landed in the pool of tears. **SPLASH!**
"I wish I hadn't cried so much!" said Alice.
There were a Duck and a Dodo, a Lory and an Eaglet, a Mouse and several other curious creatures swimming in the water. Together, they all swam to the shore.

"I think that a Caucus race would get us dry," said the Dodo.
"What's a Caucus race?" asked Alice.
"The best way to explain it is to do it," said the Dodo.
It marked out a racecourse in a circle. They started running when they liked and stopped when they liked. When they were quite dry, the race was over.

Everyone crowded around, asking who had won.

"Everybody has won, and all must have prizes," said the Dodo.

Alice found some sweets in her pocket and handed them around as prizes. Then she tried to tell them a story, but all the little animals ran away! Poor Alice was all alone again.

Alice walked on and came to a Caterpillar sitting on top of a large mushroom.

"Who are you?" it asked.

"I don't know," said Alice. "I've been changed several times."

"Explain yourself!" said the Caterpillar.

"I can't," said Alice. "I don't stay the same size for ten minutes!"

Who are you?

The Caterpillar crawled away from the mushroom.

"The left side will make you grow taller, and the right side will make you grow shorter," it said.

"Of what?" Alice asked.

"Of the mushroom," said the Caterpillar.

Alice nibbled at the mushroom pieces and, sure enough, the Caterpillar was right.

Alice walked further and came to a tiny house. She used the right-hand piece to grow smaller and she went inside.

Inside, a duchess was singing to a baby.

The cook was stirring some soup.

"Why is your cat grinning?" asked Alice.

"It's a Cheshire Cat," snapped the duchess, and she gave the baby to Alice.

"I'm going to play croquet with the Queen," said the duchess.

Alice took the baby and walked outside.

The baby grunted. It had changed into a pig! Alice put the pig down and it trotted away happily! She saw the Cheshire Cat sitting in a tree.

"Who lives here?" Alice asked.

"A Hatter and a March Hare," the Cat said. "They're both mad."

"I don't want to be with mad people," Alice remarked.

"We're all mad here," said the Cat. Then it **Vanished.**

Alice found the March Hare sitting at a long table with the Hatter and a sleepy Dormouse.

"Why is a raven like a writing desk?" asked the Hare.

"I have no idea," said the Hatter. "I want a clean cup."

They all moved on one place. Alice took the place of the March Hare.

"Once there were three little sisters," **yawned** the Dormouse, "they lived in a well and ate treacle –"

"I don't think –" began Alice.

"Then you shouldn't talk," said the Hatter.

"How rude! This is the stupidest tea party I was ever at!" cried Alice.

At last Alice found a beautiful garden. The King and Queen of Hearts came towards her, with soldiers, courtiers and the White Rabbit.

"Can you play croquet?" roared the Queen.

"Yes!" Alice cried.

It was all very strange. The balls were hedgehogs, the mallets were flamingos and the soldiers doubled over to make arches.

Soon the Queen was in a temper, shouting

"Off with his head!"

or "Off with her head!"

Then Alice saw the Cheshire Cat.
"How are you getting on?" it asked.
"They don't play fairly," Alice began.
Then the Queen saw the Cat. "Off with its head!" But, before the executioner could do anything, the Cat had disappeared.

The Queen sent Alice to meet the Gryphon and the melancholy Mock Turtle.

"Once I was a real Turtle," he said sadly. "I went to school in the sea."

The Mock Turtle and the Gryphon showed Alice how to dance the Lobster Quadrille.

Then the Mock Turtle sang a song.

"Beautiful Soup, so rich and green,
Waiting in a hot tureen!
Who for such dainties would not stoop?
Soup of the evening, beautiful Soup!
Soup of the evening, beautiful Soup!
Beau – ootiful Soo – oop!
Beau – ootiful Soo – oop!
Soo – oop of the e – e – evening,
Beautiful, beautiful Soup!"

Suddenly someone shouted,
"The trial's beginning!"
"Come on!" cried the Gryphon.

The King and Queen of Hearts were on their thrones in court, and the Knave was under arrest. The White Rabbit read the accusation:

The Queen of Hearts,
she made some tarts,
all on a summer day.

The Knave of Hearts,
he stole those tarts,
and took them
quite away!

Just then, Alice had a very strange feeling. She was starting to grow larger again.

"Call the first witness!" said
the King. The Hatter stood up.
"I'm a poor man," he trembled,
"and I hadn't begun my tea –"
"Next witness!" cried the King.
The next witness was the Cook.
"Give your evidence," said the King.
"Shan't," said the Cook.
"Next witness!" the King cried.
The White Rabbit read out the name 'Alice!'

"What do you know about this?" the King asked Alice.

"Nothing," said Alice.

"That's very important," the King told the jury.

"Unimportant, your Majesty means," said the White Rabbit.

The King scribbled in his notebook and read out, "Rule Forty-two. All persons more than a mile high to leave the court." Everybody looked at Alice.

"You just made that rule up!" said Alice.

"It's the oldest rule in the book," said the King.

"Then it ought to be Number One," said Alice.

"Consider your verdict," the King said to the jury.

"Sentence first – verdict afterwards," said the Queen.

"Stuff and nonsense!" said Alice loudly.

"Off with her head!"

the Queen shouted.

"But you're nothing but a pack of cards!" cried Alice.

The whole pack rose up into the air, and came flying at her!

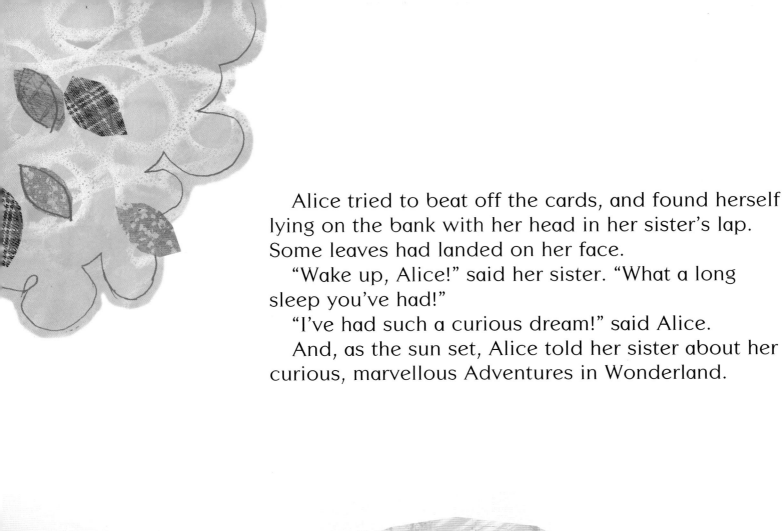

Alice tried to beat off the cards, and found herself lying on the bank with her head in her sister's lap. Some leaves had landed on her face.

"Wake up, Alice!" said her sister. "What a long sleep you've had!"

"I've had such a curious dream!" said Alice.

And, as the sun set, Alice told her sister about her curious, marvellous Adventures in Wonderland.